The people of Etheria love their Princess Adora, who is gentle and good. But there are times when Princess Adora becomes She-Ra; Princess of Power, riding Swift Wind, her winged unicorn. Those are the times when she has magic powers to defend the country against the forces of evil, or simply to help someone in trouble.

British Library Cataloguing in Publication Data
Grant, John
    Spirit is kidnapped. — (She-Ra Princess of Power.)
    I. Title   II. Davies, Robin   III. Series
    823'.914[J]   PZ7
    ISBN 0-7214-0973-3

First edition

Published by Ladybird Books Ltd Loughborough Leicestershire UK
Ladybird Books Inc Lewiston Maine 04240 USA

Spirit is kidnapped

by John Grant
illustrated by Robin Davies

Ladybird Books

When the wicked Catra set out to cause mischief to the people of Etheria, she rode on Clawdeen. Clawdeen was swift, powerful and silent as she carried Catra through field and forest. She appeared to have no equal.

But Catra was not satisfied with her giant cat. She was jealous of Princess Adora and her beautiful horse, Spirit. Spirit was also swift, but he was clever

4

as well. Adora had taught him to perform
tricks – she had even trained him to dance on his
hind legs.

Catra at last decided that there was only one
answer. She would have to capture Spirit for herself.

Her mind made up, Catra sat down to plan how she would kidnap Spirit. It would have to be done with great cunning. Wherever Adora went in Etheria she had friends. If Catra tried to capture Spirit openly, help would be on hand instantly.

Catra looked from her tower as the sun set and the shadows lengthened across Etheria. "That's it!" she cried. "I will seek the help of the witch, Shadow Weaver. With her Dark Magic, I cannot fail. And she will be as eager as I to bring pain and unhappiness to Adora by kidnapping her beloved horse."

Mounting Clawdeen, Catra set off into the night to seek Shadow Weaver. In a clearing, in the farthest depths of the Forest of Fear, Catra found the Mistress of Dark Magic.

Shadow Weaver laughed wickedly when she heard Catra's plan.

"I like it!" she cried. "That meddling Adora and her friends have ruined my plans too many times. Now, I shall have my revenge. And I have an idea of my own. Let us hold Spirit prisoner, with Adora herself as the ransom for his safe return. Queen Angella will be at our mercy if she knows that Adora is in our hands!"

"But how can we be sure that Adora will give herself up to save Spirit?" asked Catra.

"The foolish girl will do anything to save that horse," said Shadow Weaver. "It will soon be Midsummer. We will never have a better chance than then to kidnap Spirit. Clawdeen will have to help us."

It was Midsummer Day. All over Etheria the
people celebrated with games and feasting, music
and dancing. As always, Princess Adora looked
forward to the Midsummer celebrations. She was
going to be guest of honour at the fair in a village on
the edge of Whispering Wood. There would be stalls
and sideshows. Food and drink. Sport and games.

Adora rode to the fair on Spirit. She mingled with the laughing, happy crowds of people, who were glad to see her.

The centre of the village green had been kept clear for running, wrestling, archery and other contests. After a while, the village band played a loud fanfare, and everyone knew that the contests were about to begin. They crowded around the open space, ready to cheer their favourites.

11

First came the wrestling. Handsome young
peasants puffed and panted and threw each other
across the green turf. There were loud cheers for the
winners, and almost as loud cheers for the losers!

The tug-of-war ended in roars of laughter when
the rope broke, and both teams ended in a heap on
the ground!

There was another fanfare from the band. Now came the favourite item on the programme. Led by Bow, the Master Archer, a company of foresters and hunters marched on to the village green to try their skill with bow and arrow. Targets were set up, and to Adora's delight, Bow was declared champion.

The people cheered as Bow accepted his prize from the hand of Princess Adora. He thanked her, then held up his hand for silence.

"I have a favour to ask," he said.

Bow turned to the Princess.

"Everyone has heard of your horse, Spirit," he said. "And there are many tales of the wonderful things he can do. May we see some of his tricks, Your Highness?"

"Gladly," said Adora. And, while the band played, Spirit danced in time to the music. Most of the crowd only had eyes for the performing horse, as everyone clapped and cheered. But Bow's sharp eyes had noticed something – a dark cloud moving

steadily up the sky towards the sun. Surely the fair wasn't about to be spoiled by a storm? There wasn't a breath of wind. Yet still the cloud moved steadily across the blue until half of the sky was covered.

Then Bow saw that it wasn't a storm cloud. It was shadow. A thick, dark shadow was moving over the countryside, shutting out the light.

In another few moments the village green was plunged into total darkness!

As the darkness came down, people screamed. They ran in all directions. They bumped into one another. They fell over each other. And in the midst of the panic, Adora heard Spirit squeal in fright.

"Over here, Spirit!" cried Adora. She heard the hoof-beats of the terror-stricken horse, but she could see nothing. Then she heard a sinister sound. The evil laughter of Shadow Weaver.

Another voice sounded out of the darkness. "Say goodbye to Spirit!" called Catra. Clawdeen could find her way in the dark, and guided by Catra seated on her back, she quickly found Spirit. Growling and snapping at the horse's heels, she drove him from the village green and into the forest.

Slowly the shadow passed over and faded away. The people picked themselves up and began to tidy the mess of overturned stalls. The band found their instruments where they had dropped them.

But of Spirit, there was not a trace.

In a secret clearing deep in the Forest of Fear, Catra's servants had fenced in a space with stout logs. Here she brought Spirit. The gate was swung open. Clawdeen drove Spirit in, then the gate was shut firmly.

The gate clicked shut and Catra leapt into the enclosure with her groom. As soon as the groom walked towards Spirit he found himself flying through the air as Spirit lashed out with his hooves.

"I see I shall have to teach you manners!" cried
Catra. She picked up the whip dropped by the
groom and cracked it in the air. Spirit leapt back at
the sound. Catra cracked the whip again. This time
the lash flicked Spirit across the shoulder, and he
squealed in pain.

"Now!" cried Catra. "Do as you are told and you
will not be hurt. Disobey, and you will be punished!"

Catra sprang onto Spirit's back, and immediately he reared up, trying to throw her off. But Catra was an expert rider. Spirit reared and bucked, but no matter what he did, she stayed firm. Soon the horse was covered with sweat. But Catra gave him no rest. She dug in her heels and urged Spirit into a gallop round and round the small space. Whenever he showed signs of slowing down, she whipped him mercilessly.

At last Spirit could do no more. He stood, trembling with tiredness in the centre of the enclosure, his head hanging.

Catra leapt down.

"Now, I think, it's time to send for Princess Adora!"

Meanwhile, Adora and her friends were making plans to rescue Spirit.

"We can do nothing," she said, "until we know where Catra has taken him. I want everyone who caught the smallest glimpse of Catra, Clawdeen and Spirit to tell me exactly where and when. Bow, pass the word to all the woodsmen and hunters. They can tell the peasants and farmers."

"And Kowl can tell the birds and animals," said Bow.

News came in quickly. On a large map of Etheria, Adora marked each report with a cross. Soon the line of crosses stretched from the village where Spirit had been kidnapped to Whispering Wood. Beyond the Wood it crossed open country before ending on the edge of the Forest of Fear.

Greywolf brought the final word of Spirit's prison. He had bravely followed the trail into the deadly forest. Keeping under cover, he had crept close and had seen Spirit on the other side of the log fence.

A harsh croaking came from the sky. An evil-looking raven flew above their heads, with something clutched in its claws. The big black bird circled slowly.

"That is one of Catra's messengers!" cried Adora.

The raven gave one more croak, then it dropped the object it was holding. It was a small, shining metal tube. It fell into the long grass. Bow picked it up and unscrewed the end, to find a paper inside.

"It is a message from Catra," he said.

"GREETINGS, PRINCESS ADORA. YOUR FOUR-LEGGED FRIEND IS WELL AND IN GOOD HANDS. I INVITE YOU TO BE MY GUEST. COME ALONE. THE SAFETY OF SPIRIT DEPENDS ON THAT. MY MESSENGER WILL COME FOR YOUR REPLY AT THIS TIME TOMORROW."

The message was sealed with Catra's cat sign.

Adora stood looking down at the message. "Yes, I will go alone," she said. "But at once, before Catra expects me."

"I will come with you, as your bodyguard," said Bow.

"No," said Adora. "I must do as Catra says."

"Then, at least let me accompany you as far as the edge of the Forest of Fear," insisted Bow.

To herself, Adora thought, "This is really a task for She-Ra, Princess of Power. But, She-Ra without Swift Wind would be suspicious. I must do this as an ordinary girl...to begin with, anyway."

Madame Razz came swooping along on Broom. "You're a very brave girl," she cried, "but a little magic can come in useful, I always say." And she held out a long cloak. "This is a cloak of invisibility. All you have to do is put it on, blink twice...and you're invisible!"

"How do I become visible again?" asked Adora.

"Blink twice and take it off," said Madame Razz. "Goodbye and good luck!"

26

Mounted behind Bow on his horse, Arrow, Adora set off. Late in the day they reached the edge of the Forest of Fear. Adora dismounted.

"Good luck!" called Bow, as she made her way into the shadow of the evil wood. "I will wait here until you return."

Adora waved her hand, then turned to follow a twisting path that led into the depths of the forest. It was almost dark when she came to the edge of the trees. It was not the end of the Forest of Fear, but the edge of a wide clearing. In the centre of the clearing was an enclosure built of stout logs. And, inside it, Adora could see the white coat of her horse shining in the dusk.

Spirit caught Adora's scent. He whinnied in greeting. Adora heard the voice of Catra. "You're wasting your breath, my fine friend. No one will ever find you here!"

Adora found a sheltered place deep among the
trees. She drew her Sword of Power and placed it
on the ground, ready. Then she wrapped herself in
Madame Razz's cloak and lay down to sleep.

She woke while it was still dark, although day-
break was not far away. Now it was time for She-Ra
to take over. Holding the Sword aloft, she cried:
    "FOR THE HONOUR OF GRAYSKULL!"

In an instant, Princess Adora became She-Ra, Princess of Power!

That was the first part of her plan.

For the next part she had to get as close as possible to Spirit without being seen. If Clawdeen were on the prowl, even the darkness would not conceal her.

She must use Madame Razz's magic cloak!

She-Ra was not the only one awake and about in the Forest of Fear. Catra was so excited at the thought of capturing Spirit *and* Adora that she could not sleep. She just had to have another look at her prisoner. She rose from her bed, left her tower, and rode swiftly on Clawdeen.

Spirit snorted in fear as he caught the scent of the great cat. He backed into the far corner of the enclosure when Catra climbed on to the fence for a better look. She strained her eyes. Yes, the white horse was still there. Today she would teach him some special tricks!

Catra laughed a wicked laugh!

Wrapping the cloak of invisibility around her, She-Ra blinked twice. And nothing happened! She was still visible! She could see in the starlight her hand holding the Sword! But, where was the cloak? She could feel it against her body...but she couldn't see it!

Madame Razz had done it again! It was a cloak of invisibility, sure enough; but it was the cloak itself which disappeared...not the person wearing it!

She-Ra turned the cloak visible again and hung it on a tree branch. Now, she would have to come into the open, and act fast.

She raced across the clearing and reached the enclosure just as Catra was climbing into the saddle. A blaze of mystic light shone from the Sword. And Catra suddenly found herself astride, not Spirit the white horse, but Swift Wind the winged unicorn!

Catra screamed! What had happened? The white horse was gone. And in its place was a winged unicorn. That meant only one thing. That meddling She-Ra had taken a hand in rescuing Spirit, and had left Swift Wind in his place.

Catra made to dismount, but she was too late.

She-Ra's voice rang out. "Now, Swift Wind, you can take Catra for a ride!"

Dawn was breaking, and in the first light of morning Swift Wind soared on powerful wings up and up above the Forest of Fear. Catra held on as tightly as she could as Swift Wind soared and swooped.

She-Ra called from the ground far below, "It's a beautiful morning, Catra! I hope you enjoyed your ride."

Then, Swift Wind dived fast towards the ground. At the last moment, he spun round so that Catra lost her hold and fell into a tangle of bushes.

As Catra vanished into the undergrowth she shouted, "Clawdeen! Come quickly!"

With a snarl, the great cat bounded out from among the trees. Swift Wind had landed in the clearing, but Clawdeen was between him and She-Ra. She-Ra made to run round Clawdeen, but the cat moved too quickly.

She charged with a savage roar, and She-Ra sprinted for the cover of the Forest. As Clawdeen

raced after She-Ra, Swift Wind rose into the air. He must rescue his beloved mistress. But there was nowhere among the tangled treetops where he could land. She-Ra must reach open country. She ran back along the path she had come by.

Close behind her she heard the sound of Clawdeen as she followed hard on her heels.

The path twisted and turned. Clawdeen was out of sight — but not far behind.

Suddenly, She-Ra turned a corner and there was Madame Razz's cloak where she had left it hanging on a tree. She stopped and unhooked the cloak from the branch. She put it on, blinked twice, and the cloak vanished from sight. A low branch overhung the path. She-Ra hung up the cloak on it and spread it out above the path. Clawdeen bounded round the corner, saw She-Ra, and with a loud snarl, leapt at her.

Next moment she was on the ground as the invisible cloak wrapped itself around her.

As Clawdeen fought to free herself from
something she couldn't see, She-Ra raced on
through the trees. Soon she came to a clearing
where she found Swift Wind waiting for her. In a
moment they were skimming across the treetops.
Close to the edge of the forest they came to earth.
She-Ra became Adora once more and Swift Wind
became Spirit.

Bow was waiting as he had promised, and together they rode home. A great crowd had gathered to greet them, and everyone rejoiced at the safe return of Spirit.

"How did you do it?" everyone wanted to know.

"I was really very lucky," said Adora. "Spirit was extremely brave. And, of course, I could have done nothing without the help of Madame Razz and her magic."

Everyone cheered again, and as Bow looked at Spirit, he could have sworn that the horse turned his head and winked at Adora!